Blue & Grey

Flairs and Glairs
Publication House

"Blue & Grey"

ISBN No: " 978-93-91302-62-7"
1st Edition
Language – English and Hindi

Flairs and Glairs
Publication House
Regd. Under MSME Act.

Disclaimer

This is a work of fiction and solely represent the thoughts of the corresponding authors of the articles. Our editors have tried their best to edit the content of all the authors and check the plagiarism.
All the write-ups in this book are unique and are only published in this book.
In case any plagiarism or error is found, only the author is responsible alone, and not the publisher or the Compilers.

Cover Designing and Book Formatting
Shubham Shah and Ishani Agarwal

Acknowledgement

I would like to acknowledge the enormous help given to me in creating this book. I extend a special thanks to all the co-authors for being patient and believing in me. Also, the whole team of flairs and Glairs, for giving me such an amazing opportunity.

This book is Dedicated to all those people who change the lives of others by living as an example and by empowering others towards greatness. And to the one person who has empowered me, and never stopped believing in me. Thank you. I hope each reader finds solace in the pages of this book.

Co Authors

Shubham Shah (Founder Flairs and Glairs)
Ishani Agarwal (Co-Founder Flairs and Glairs)
Shivangi Jaiswal (Project Head)
Sameeksha Kalra (Compiler)

1. Simran Bhandari
2. Shivanshi Ahlawat
3. Avantika Thakur
4. Yashasvi Mehlawat
5. Noordeep Singh
6. Japneet Chandoak
7. Sushmita Singh
8. Samridhi Jairath
9. Sarisha Singh
10. Chandni Sachdeva
11. Jasnoor Arora
12. Arshpreet Kaur Dharwal
13. Ishita Kaur
14. M. Shalini Mary
15. Dhruv Kapoor
16. Ritvika Rathore
17. Harsh Dabarthala
18. Sangeeta Chauhan
19. Manpreet Bhullar
20. Modern Likhari

Shubham Shah

(Founder- Flairs and Glairs)

Shubham Shah, an entrepreneur at "Flairs & Glairs" a brand with dynamics in events organizing and cultural educational pan INDIA, is a 26yrs old guy who recently has entered the digital platform of imprinting emotions. He has initiated with his own open mic platform to help budding poets and aspiring writers under his brand named as "Teekhe Zasbaaat"

He is a commerce graduate from the Bhagalpur City of Bihar. He states Writing has impersonated him since childhood and he has now been writing for over a decade!
Cooking, on the other hand, is his passion! He also mentions, trying out new things just tickles him!
When asked sir, Why SPICY EMOTIONS?
He smiled and added, “agar jasbaat teekhe na ho toh wo jasbaat kahan” Spices are all that blends! So do his words!
As a chef, he presents to you his dish! Hot and freshly served! Taste it! Feel it! Enjoy it! You can also find his writing in the Book “Teekhe Zasbaaat” and 50+ Co-authored anthologies. With his passion to explore opportunities across Platforms, he is working with keen devotion and We wish him all the very best for his future ventures.
He is Featured in the International Magazine DeMode for his upcoming solo novel.
He is Approved by Ne8x for its Lit Fest, and is a Golden Star Awards 2020 Winner.
He is a India Book of Records Holder for his Anthology Satrang, and has the Grandmaster title by Asia Book of Records, for the same.
He has also been featured in Prabhat Khabar, Dainik Jagran, and a lot of other Newspapers in Bihar for his achievements.
He has been a proud co-author to
India Book Of Records (Title- Black)
World Book Of Records (Title -15 Wonders of Poetries)
India Book Of Records (Title - Aaina)
Vajra World Records Holder (Title - Gustakhi Maaf Hai)
High Range of Records Holder (Title - Gustakhi Maaf Hai)
Indian Book of Records
(Title - Road from Worst to Best)

Share your reviews on his

INSTAGRAM
@spicy_emotions
@shubham4shah

Or via email on
shubham2shah@gmail.com

To stay tuned to his work and opportunities follow his business Handles

INSTAGRAM FACEBOOK YOUTUBE

@flairsandglairs
@teekhezasbaaat

WEBSITE:
https://flairsandglairs.in/
https://flairsandglairs.com/

Ishani Agarwal

(Co-Founder- Flairs and Glairs)

Ishani Agarwal hails from the City of Joy, Kolkata.
She is the co-founder of her Community "Teekhe Zasbaaat" and Flairs and Glairs Publication.
Been a Compiler for 45+ Anthologies, she is in the process for more. Co-authored in 150+ Anthologies. She is a India Book of Records Holder, a Vajra World Records Holder, a High Range of Records Holder, an OMG Book of Records Holder, a Bravo Record holder, a Forever Star Book of World Records and an Indian Book of Records Holder.
Approved by Ne8x for its Lit Fest 2020, and Literary Icon 2020. Also a Golden Star Awards Winner 2020.
She has also been awarded with India Star Republic Award 2021, a part of She Awards by Awards Arc and Winner of Nari Samman 2021 by Literoma.

She is also selected as Best Achiever of the Year by AwardsArc and Most Challenging Compiler Award by Spectrum Awards.
She got her first solo Published,a solo Compilation consisting of first 750 contents of hers, titled "Hand That Burnt While Healing".

She has been featured by the National Magazine "Taree Zameen Par" with the title 'unstoppable'.
Also featured in the International Magazine DeMode for her upcoming solo novel, she is proud to write on social issues, and is happy with the love she is receiving.
Connect with her on Instagram: @Ishani_agarwal_quotes / @compilations_so_far

Shivangi Jaiswal
(Project Head)

Shivangi Jaiswal is a Content Writer from Kolkata. Executive Head at "Flairs & Glairs" brand with dynamics in events organizing and cultural educational pan INDIA She is a B. Com Honors graduate. Certified in Stocks & Short Selling as well as Certified in Digital Marketing. Been a keen student, she has recently been Certified for learning Spanish Language. She is a writer by day and a reader by night. Been a Complier of 32+ Anthologies, and in process for more, also Co- authored 120+ anthologies. Shivangi is an old soul with young eyes, a vintage heart, and a beautiful mind."

You can follow her work:
Instagram
@the_knockingvibe
@house_of_compilations

(1)

The sky was full of stars,
So, lit
So beautiful,
by splendor of the moon.

Looking up in the sky,
I see your face.
Your passionate love
have made me so pure.

Because in the garden
of my heart, you grew
a heart with your love.
Kissing my soul, and
making it heal.

The two great eyes slay,
and beauty struck a spark
between them.

Sameeksha Kalra
[Compiler]

Sameeksha Kalra is a 20 year old writer, hobby baker and artist. She is a Bachelor's student at Ggdsd College, Chandigarh. She completed her schooling from Birla Balika Vidyapeeth Bits Pilani, Rajasthan. Being a bibliophile and a passionate writer, it is her quest for the true meaning of existence which takes her to the altar of renowned poets and writers. Books have not only empowered her but also given her a vision. For her literature mirrors life and there can be no better medium than this to express oneself. She is a Published Co-author in two Anthologies.
INSTA: @sameeksha_kalra

Our Discrete Universe

We are connected yet so far,
I wonder why we are at war.
I can never let you come so close,
Cause the last time my heart almost froze.
We are just like the sun and moon,
You may not realise my sacrifices soon.
But Here I am, burning for your sake,
How could you be so fake.
The moon and stars are always blended
Together in this enormous sky,
While my love for you shall never die.
Me being the sun,
Will always wish for the moon and stars
To stick together like you and her.
We may have never been meant to be together,
But we shall always glow in our discrete universe forever.

Forevermore

The red old sun was sinking to the dark,
Round the corner you could see its spark;
He was there waiting, waiting for more,
While his tears were rolling off the shore;
The waves were chasing him back into the past,
For the promises he made, and the memories he lost;
His heart was willing to say it all,
All the stories he could recall;
She was his love, and will always be.

The weight it holds now is no more than
That of a falling leaf,
The sadness though is very brief;
Years have passed, now it is nothing but a blur,
Sometimes though he still misses her.

An Ode To The Inevitable - Love

Love is a four letter word that rules the world.
It is the ultimate source of immense pleasure
as well as the deepest pain.
It creates magic as well as havoc.
It's not a long story,
Just my thoughts on a small piece of paper
That comprises volumes of love of a dreamer,
Thoughts flowing in the space.

When a person tells you that he cares for you, loves you;
Why in the world do we lose ourselves,
Why do we start searching for love from another soul,
Why do we crave for that persons touch,
Can something so real, so magical and captivating
Exist between two people.
I don't believe in magic, but if it does
I think it's in between the space that two people hold.
The magic that sweeps you off your feet
And puts you in a state of ecstasy.

Some people tell me,
Loving another person is very difficult
Because no one overcomes disappointment.
But for me loving someone is very easy.
Even when I tried hard not to I couldn't help but to love.
No matter how much I wanted to be disappointed,
I could not, for me love overcomes everything.

And love doesn't diminish, or just stop existing
Because someone does not love you back.
In fact it sort of makes that love real;
For not wanting anything in return.

It's all about being able to give it to the right one,
In the right way.
We are all humans and love is inevitable to us. '
The falling', 'The breaking', and ' The healing'
Is what's supposed to happen to us.
And there is no escaping that.

No doubt love is the most beautiful, peaceful feeling
I have ever felt,
But at the same time it feels so dark,
Empty and terrifying.
I bet I can hear every part of my soul shattering
On the very thought of losing you.
I wish someday I find someone;
Someone I can love more than you.
Just so I can miss you a little less.

Whenever I try to feel a little emotion,
Even the ones I had put out a long time ago.
Someone comes and wrecks me over.
The present me is maybe strong enough to handle it,
But the 11 year old inside me wants to cry
And make a fuss over it,
To why this is happening,
Over and over again.

As a kid; I tried and tried,
And finally did learn to shut people out,
But the 20 year old me feels
The need to hold onto someone,
But somewhere inside has that fear of abandonment,
That fear of falling again, and not being able to stand up again..

There was an old man walking up a hill,
And a man coming towards him on a horse
The horse jolted past the old man,
And he somehow managed to dodge them.

He asked the man, shouting from behind,
'Where are you going?'
The man on the horse replied,
'I don't know', ask the horse.

The horse represents our fears and trauma.
They keep guiding us throughout our lives.
We keep going around and around,
Without knowing where we are going,
And end up in a situation where
We can't even answer a simple question,
"Where are you going?"

Simran Bhandari

Simran Bhandari is a Bachelor's student at GGDSD College, Chandigarh. She is a budding writer and believes that if any kind of magic exists, it is in the space between two people. For her, literature is the only way one can not only save themselves but also another, in every way a person can possibly be saved. As a co-author, this is her first venture.

INSTA: @kyu_yaar_simran

Tumhe btane ka Mann krta hai
Woh sab kuch,
Jo humare baare mein samajh liya hai Maine!
Mai tumhe apni adhoori neendon mein chhupati hu
Tumhare hisse ke Safar bhi mai khud hi kar jati hu!
Mai ghanto baith kar likhti hu
Par kuch lafz hi bol pati hu!
Sab puchte hain mujhse, ki kahan kho aayi hu khudko
Par tumhe btane ka mann krta hai...
Ki iss gumshudayi mein sukoon Kitna hai!
Tumhe btane ka Mann krta hai
Ki tum na...tareef ki latt jaise ho
Har harf ke sath sir par chadh jate ho!
Tumhe btane ka mann krta hai...
Ki tumhari khamoshi mujhe atpati si lgti hai
Tumpar baatein bohot jach-ti Hain!
Tumhe btane ka mann krta hai
Ki tum mere liye kisi itwaar se kamm nahi ho
Tumhara intezar mujhe bohot be-sabri se hota hai!
Par tum samajhte hi nahi
Ki mujhme jo bhi kuch khaas hai
Wo tumhi se toh milta hai!!!

Kya tumhe bhi lgta hai ye?
Ki baarishon mein nashey mile hote hain
Aise nashey jo rok lete hain musafiron ko ghar pohochne se
Aise nashey jo maikado mein baithe qafiron ko bhi
ghar lauta dete hain
Aise nashey jo aashna ko bhi humnava bna jate hain
Aise nashey jo harf ko bhi dastaan bna jate hain

Kya tumhe bhi lgta hai ye?
Ki tum bhi in baarishon ke nashey ki tarah ho
Aise, jaise tumhare na hone tak bhi sab theek sa hi tha
Par tumhare hone ka ehsaas hone ke baad
tum in haatho se chhoot hi nahi rhe....
Aise, jaise tumhari darkaar ek kaynaati masla ho gyi hai

Kya tumhe bhi lgta hai ye?
Mujhse pucho agar toh mujhe lgta hai
Ki baarishon mein nashey bhi tum hi milate ho!
Kaliyoon ko apna kayal kar jane ke liye!!
Hai na ??

Sometimes, the thoughts of you holding my hand,
Interrupts me while speaking.
In my mind, I sound like that pause before one starts to cry.
But people, they say I sound poetic.

Sometimes, I feel the willingness in my bones to please your demons. Have them impressed by the way I misbehave with your angels.
In my mind, it sounds like a death wish.
But my heart, it will love you and the most terrible thing you ever did.

Cause the 5'11" of you, has had me overshadowed with love.
The 5'11" of you, has had me consumed, inch by inch.
The 5'11" of you, has had me absorbed, drop by drop.
The 5'11" of you, has had me gone crazy.
The 5'11" of you, has had me whisper my cravings for you, in your ears, without the use of words.
The 5'11" of you, has had me trap my world, in the space between our fingers.
The 5'11" of you, has had me burn in a slow fire, eliminating the anxiousness down my throat.
The 5'11" of you, has had me smile through my eyes. As if I have met myself after ages.
The 5'11" of you, has had me drawn towards you as if you were a firefly.
Come, have me. I'm yours for taking

Agar khol du khudko parat-dar-parat tumhare samne,
Mujhko usi nigah se dekh paoge kya?
Pyaar to nahi keh paungi apna tumhe kabhi,
Fir bhi jab tootu to mera sukoon ban paoge kya?
Agar bta du use tabah krne ki apni har wo na-paak chahat jo maine khudko bhi nahi btayi,
Fir bhi apni paak mohabbat mujhpe zaya kar paoge kya?

Dekha to bohoto ne hai mujhe, Tum padh paoge kya?
Hath mai pakad liya karungi tumhara,
Pal thoda theher ke meri aankho mein dekh paoge kya?
Sama lungi tumhara saara dukh ka bhaar mai khud mein,
Fir bhi meri neeyat ka aadar kar paoge kya?
Jata nahi paungi ki tum kya ho mere liye,
Kya fir bhi mere sath khade ho paoge kya?
Masoomiyat ko har kisi ne apne fareb ka karan bnaya hai,
Tum use apne pyaar ka karan bna paoge kya?

Khuda kare tujhe ishq chadhe
Uss ishq mein tu bhi khud ko kho jaye!
Kehni chaho har baat use
Woh baatein tere ashq ho jaye!
Ishq hi Teri bandegi ho
Uss bandegi mein tera har ek dastoor bebas ho jaye!
Har pal rahe tujhe uske deedar ki aarzoo
Uss aarzoo mein tera jeena dushwaar ho jaye!
Tu bhi use apni bekhudi ki daleelen de
Uske jalal ke aage teri har ek daleel fanaa ho jaye!
ulfat mein hi tujhe taskeen mile
Woh faqat hasrat hi reh jaye!
Uski qurbat tujhe laazmi lage
Uska inkaar teri tabahi ho jaye!
Khuda kare tujhe ishq chadhe
Uss ishq mein tu bhi khud ko kho jaye!

Shivanshi Ahlawat

Shivanshi Ahlawat, just got done with her MSc. Biotechnology from DAV College, Sector-10, Chandigarh. She likes to dance in her free time. She likes to write quotes, haikus that are inspired by her day-to-day routine. As a co-author, this is her second venture and much more will follow. INSTA: @she_van_she

Maybe I'm wise now,

Or a lil more nice now,

Maybe wee bit polite now,

Someone's guiding light now,

Maybe I'm with some flaws now,

But perfection got no laws now,

& Maybe,

Maybe I'm more human now.

The Enigma

Just look at
How the 'stars' as sequins,
Are sewed to the pitch-black fabric
We see as 'space',
I wonder who dons this beautiful attire
We see as a 'night sky'.

Your arrival was like
The rain,
You casted out the dusty skies of
My mind.

Your aura is like
The rainbow,
Your seven hues promise nothing but
Eternal warmth and elation.

Your smile is like,
The sun,
All radiant and contagious.

Your soul,
So moon-like,
That sends my heart into fathoms deep
Serenity

Avantika Thakur

Born on 24-03-1995, in Hoshiarpur, Punjab, Avantika Thakur did her schooling from St. Joseph's Convent School, Hoshiarpur. She completed her B.A.(Hons.) and M.A. English from Government College, Hoshiarpur. Later she pursued her B.Ed. from Government College of Education, Chandigarh, where she got numerous opportunities to nurture and showcase her hidden talents. She won various competitions in the field of drama and even won first prize in the Youth Festival (Creative Story Writing Competition). Since childhood, she had a keen interest in stories n fiction. Her favourite writers are W. Shakespeare and Sophie Kinsella. For her, imagination can make wonders happen and stories give the strength to keep up with the struggles of life for yet another day.
INSTA: @avantika_thakur

The Fortune Ticket

"So gaya yeh jahaan, so gaya.... Aasamaa" song was playing on the cab radio. Latika was sitting on the back seat with a briefcase, waiting for the cab driver to come back from the tea stall. She kept looking at the car-watch impatiently.

It was around 7:30 in the evening, the sun had set and the horizon could be clearly seen as a dim pinkish shade of the sky at the end of the highway. The driver returned and cab was on the road again. Latika looked out of the window of the car. The moving car made her feel that the fields on the roadside moved just like happiness was to move with her again. The dimming daylight took her into a flashback...

In a small town of Madhya Pradesh, Latika lived with her parents. Her father worked in a cloth company and her mother was a housewife. She was the only child of her parents and her father tried his best to give her a life of her dreams. Latika was 13 years old when her mother died in a LPG cylinder blast at her house, while she was at school and her father was at work. After her mother's death, Latika's father started drinking a lot. He did not care about anyone or anything anymore. Succumbed to his drinking habit, his work and personal life suffered a great deal. He even lost his job because he messed up many orders.

Latika was ignored a lot during her teenage. She didn't have anyone to talk to. She missed her mother and even her father. Most difficult part of her day was walking the distance from her school to her house. Many boys teased and picked on her. When she complained to her father, he didn't pay any heed. Helplessly, she looked at him with tears in her eyes. She wondered why her father turned his back on her in such a phase.

One day, at school, Latika got into a fight with a boy who called her father, "*bewadaa*". Frustrated Latika punched him in the face. The boy slapped her head and pulled her pigtails. Latika screamed but still managed to kick him in the stomach. The boy bent and she pushed him away, but the boy hit his head on the corner of the table and started bleeding. Panicked and confused Latika ran out. The other boys chased her out of the school until she boarded a moving bus. Panting and frightened Latika was unable to understand anything. All she knew was she had just fled away from most dreadful situation of her life. She sat on a vacant seat and fell asleep as the wind hit her exhausted face.

Latika woke up when the bus came to a forced halt. She got out of the bus and looked at her surroundings. The board of a halwai's shop said '*Manikpur* '. She had never heard of this place. She thought about her recent experience which got her goose bumps. She decided not to go back. Just 15 years old, Latika didn't know what she would do in this unfamiliar city.

Hungry and tired, she went to the halwai's shop and bought some '*pakoras*' for Rs 10(the only money in her pocket). Walking around in the school uniform, she came across a lady who seemed in her mid – thirties. The lady asked the lost girl where she lived. The girl started wailing in front of her. The lady consoled her after listening to her tragic loss. The lady asked her to accompany her to an orphanage.

Though Latika started living in the orphanage but she never liked it there. The caretaker of the orphanage, Miss Baagchi, was an evil lady who made the girls work day and night and fed them low-nutrition diet.

One day Latika was cleaning the entrance steps when she heard a voice," Buy these lottery tickets, win 1 crore. Try your luck, win 1 crore". Latika stopped and turned around to see a man wearing torn clothes, hanging a board full of lottery tickets in front of his cycle. The road was uneven and he was

unable to ride his bicycle properly. He tried to speed up but it resulted in his fall. Latika ran to help him up. She collected the scattered lottery tickets and gave them back to him. The man was hurt in the arm. She gave him water to clean his wound. The man smiled and gave her a lottery ticket as blessing. She smiled after seeing the ticket and went back to her chores. As soon as Latika reached the entrance of the orphanage, Miss Baagchi started shouting at her. Latika hid her lottery ticket in her apron and resumed her work.

Few months after this incident, Latika was called by Miss Baagchi in her office. There was a man who looked familiar but she was unable to recall him. He claimed to be a good friend of her father.

After her sudden disappearance, her father and he searched for her everywhere and she turned out to be nowhere but here. Due to his drinking habits, her father was suffering from severe illness and wished to see her. He had come to take Latika along with him. But Miss Baagchi denied him the permission to take Latika. She asked for Rs20,000/- for her release. The man requested the lady to send the girl as she was the only child of that dying man. But that greedy hag didn't let him take her.

She locked the mewling girl in her room and refused to give her any food. After two days, the room was opened and Latika was fed half portion of the one-time meal. Latika was now given more chores than before. As soon as she came to 'cleaning of the entrance steps', she remembered that it was the day the result of the lottery was to be announced. She waited for the chance and escaped from the orphanage.

She reached the office where lottery tickets were being checked and winners were being rewarded. She looked at that fortune changing ticket for one last time and prayed. With trembling hands, this 17 year old girl gave her ticket to the man at the counter. With a smile, the man looked at her eagerly-waiting-for-some-miracle-to-happen tired face and said,"Mubarak ho, beti! 3rd prize…. 10 Lakh". Latika was taken aback after hearing these words. She got all numb. The man asked her to wait for an hour as she would be given half of the prize money right away and the rest of it after a month.

"So gaya yeh jahaan. So Gaya…. Aasmaa" was still playing on the cab radio. She was sitting in the cab with the briefcase full of 5 lakh rupees. She was going back to her father. With every mile she crossed, she felt adrenaline rush. She was nervous about facing her old man after so many years. She was thinking of her previous times with her happy family and now she was certain that she would bring those happy days through that briefcase.

Suddenly, the screeching of tires was heard and the car got out of control. Accompanied with the loud sound of "*thud*", the car flipped once... twice.... thrice... hitting the ground and everything felt broken. The cab met with an accident while saving the drunk driver of the opposite lane and was hit by a speeding truck behind it. All glass shattered into pieces. The briefcase broke and money appeared to be falling from the sky. Latika wanted to move but her body couldn't. She couldn't feel a thing. Her whole life flashed in front of her eyes with the falling money… her mother, her father, a happy little Latika and the lottery ticket that was to change her fortune forever. With these last images, she felt her soul leaving her body... rising in the sky, along the fumes, against the falling money.

Yashasvi Mehlawat

She is an aspiring writer. A graduate from Gargi College, university of Delhi. A person with great belief in creative aspect coming from within the heart, she is a meticulous person with her passion in reading and creating magic with her creative caliber. For her, creativity lies within and comes from one's heart. As she says that she's just a wanderer in the search for tranquility, with her calm persona she's sure to leave you captivated with her flare in writing. As a co- author it's her first venture to a delightful experience ahead.

INSTA: @theartsywriter_ @yashasvi_mehlawat

Not a Goodbye

It seems like a snap of a finger,
Where at first it was because of you I smiled a little wider, gleaming with happiness,
To now where I ponder upon the thought of just your shadow being next to my door,
Where now even your shadow seems to fade,
I never knew with the moments of unbound happiness there was a goodbye waiting in disguise,
For which now I wish,
I could see you one more time walking through the door,
Wish I could gaze at you a bit longer,
Hold you a bit closer,
Where every minute would be all so precious,
Where I could just be with you without looking back,
Where happiness has no bounds,
In a world where there are no goodbyes.

Unapologetically Me

"Enough", you've had enough"
Was something I had to say out loud to myself or what my body had to say to me from all the exhaustion.
To all the years that passed by,
To the times I used to look at the mirror, never smiling.
From the moment I knew of the word body or the word me, leading to relentless comparisons, never realising to where the tenderness was all lost,
Where of all the children "I'm the best" was a phrase too difficult to believe in for me.
To being trapped into self-loathing and self-doubting that clipped on to my lungs leaving them caged,
Where I stood barely breathing, just to survive,
Where every night I found my heart all so heavy, turning from one side to another, pretending to sleep, while deep inside I knew that all I did was stuff myself with all the criticisms...
It is now that I realise it came from no one else but me.
All these years I've looked down upon no one else but me. All these years I looked into the mirror searching for perfection forgetting the horizons within me, of the beautiful mess I am, of the capacities I hold.
Through the years I've been working to be someone I was looking for,
For every time I looked at the mirror, I never embraced the path from where I began,
To where i am now.
To the all the years of exhaustion, with the guilt to be myself,
To the times, now when I tell myself to look at the mirror, to come out of the shackles, to look at the new rays of energy within me for new the possibilities I built.
For now I strive to be unapologetically me.

Through The Shadows I Rise

As the day comes to an end,
I find myself looking up to the ceiling
Feeling trapped within these four walls I call home.
Trying to escape my own emotions of how I hide them from the people that make my home.
Looking for comfort within them, failing to realise even they've had their own.
Throughout my childhood I grew up being fascinated by my own shadow trying to leave it behind,
the sight of it following me haunted me,
little did i realise it was just me.
As the years went by this fascination seemed to be long lost leaving me to wonder.
will it still follow me?
since when did it grow taller than me leaving me to lose my very own identity.
Minding each step I take ahead, minding every action of how it might look in the shadows,
Of what people perceive.
Soon to realise, all my life I've been haunted by my own ghosts,
Of my actions and fears failing to realise the capacities I hold.
At last when now I look deep down my own shadow rather looking at my own self
trying to accept of who I am , of all the imperfections I hold.
As I see the darker parts of me and strive to grow, leaving these shadows to a standstill where now they no longer grow.

As The Silence Breaks

All my life I kept hiding,
Covering the bruises deep within me,
I kept mum, for all I was asked to do.
Every time I tried expressing, you were the one to shut me up.
All I had to say, was left swallowed in me.
Little did I know to what it might lead
My soul was all ruptured, to now my wounds bleed.
All my life I lived like the living dead, gripping on to my fears,
To live seemed oblivion... Where all I did was to exist.
I had a lot to say, all bottled in me
To a rage it might lead.
To set free was all that came to my mind,
But my soul being caged all I could see...
Today I promise to let all the fears lose
Where today I shout my lungs out
To be able to heal my wound.
No longer will I hide the scars left dark
Where now I turn them into galaxies my own,
To path of endless hopes it leads
Being my own strength is a promise to keep
No matter how dark the path might be
I dare to stand alone
Leading to an unstoppable me!

Concentric Circles

Have you ever looked at the trees and wondered how the circles that surrounds them in tell their stories, their stories of life...
Just like that the concentric circle of life tells mine,
The innumerable lives I've lived some scarred, some beautiful, some being happy, some full of sorrows and regret... They say marriages are made in heaven, mine was just in sorrow and despair...
Where my family justified his brutality
Where they wanted me to hold on; I tried, tried to hold on, to make him believe in love... as in this judgmental society to get your own happiness is a spinning ride of impossibilities, but all I did went in vain
Where at night he blamed me for all his downfalls, raising his hand on me, was his only escape and how it would give him a strange satisfaction to look down on me and talk about the other woman who was his paradise...
The toxicity gripped my soul leaving it in emptiness
Leaving me in pieces, fallen apart difficult to put together for me to stand... Since one day I decided not to live for them, yes the society and rather for myself
For just letting myself be, to breathe and start afresh...
Today all my sorrows seem to fade where I get to be with the love of my life away from the past...at an unusual age, yes at 60.
Where now all that matters is my happiness!
As I write my name next to his, being pronounced as husband and wife,
It looks like a dream, too good to be true
But it's him, all that matters at last...
With his unspoken words telling me he will never let me go, the touch of his hands making me believe he'll never let me fall apart,
Where all my life I see with him
With him it feels just right
Where there's never too late for love to arrive!

Noordeep

Noordeep Singh is doing Bachelors in Science from Dav College, Chandigarh. He is quite a weeb; loves watching anime and a k-pop fan. He is passionate about writing and also tries to better himself in the art of expressing with words.
As a co-author, this is his first ever venture but it isn't the last as he has a dream of becoming a well-known novelist.

INSTA: @noordeep015

Heartening Smile

Adam crossed the road, walking to the flower stall. He bought beautiful blue flowers. He knew she liked blue flowers and he wanted to buy the forget-me-nots for her as they were rare around there area. He remembered the first time they had met two years ago at a party where he found out that she was in his college. They become friends in no time. He smelled the flowers he had just bought. He smiled as he got in his car.
He drove his car, returning back to the city. He looked at the park on his right. He stopped his car and got out of it. He looked at people and couples walking in the park, in the same park he had proposed to her. She had said yes and he couldn't explain how her answer made butterflies fly in his stomach and his cheeks blush. He looked at the park, every couple in the park reminded him of both of them.

"You took a year, idiot. Though, thank you for not taking two years." She said and hugged him tightly, almost crying in his shoulder.
He chuckled, hugging her back and said, "How was I supposed to know you love me?" She just nudged him softly telling him that he should notice some hints. He remembered it.

He got back in his car as he couldn't stay here. A tear rolled down his cheeks. He started his car and drove to a house in the city. He got out with his flowers. He walked to a man and gave him the car keys. He took the money from him in cash.

He took a bus, holding the flowers in his hands. He chuckled and said, "You sure want a wedding with blue and white flower decor. We would have to wait for it now."

Adam got off the bus and walked into the hospital. He took the lift to the third floor. He pushed the door open as he saw her lying unconscious on the bed.

“Hey, Eve.” He said, placing the flowers in the vase; next to her bed. “The final operation is today and you’ll be all fine by tomorrow.” He ran his hand through her dark hairs. She had met with an accident three months ago and hadn’t woken up since. Doctors told him that she is in a coma and she might not make it out. He didn’t believe what they said. She had little chance of surviving.
He went to the reception and paid for the operation. He used to think money was everything and over the months he had sold his house, his car and worked over time, saving money for her. The doctors took her to the ICU. “Eve, you promised. You’ll die with me of old age in a house with our kids beside us. You can’t break it.” He whispered standing in front of the door.

After a few long hours the doctors came out. “She will make it; if she wakes up this week then she’ll be better in no time.” His smile grew wider and thanked them. He walked into the room and sat next to her, holding her hand.
Next day, He was sleeping but even in his sleep he whispered, “Please, live. I love you, Eve.”
“I love you too, Adam.” She said, placing her hand on his head, softly rubbing his hairs. When he woke up and saw her smiling at him, he cried like a baby, hugging her tightly. His heart was at ease, he knew no amount of money would make him feel the way her smile made him feel. “I love you. Please marry me as soon as possible, Eve.” He said looking at her.
She giggled and said, “Really, Proposing me in a hospital? Yeah, that’s every girl’s dream.” She smiled as he chuckled and smiled back at her. She pulled him closer and said, “The answer is yes.” They kissed each other lovingly.

The Boy's Growth

He ran and he ran faster crossing two boys. He sprinted and crossed another boy, reclaiming the third position as his own. I had come here to see him win, I had seen him practice the whole month in the park in front of my house. When I asked him why he was doing that, he had answered that he had a race at his school and he wanted to win it. After that day I had seen him getting faster day by day. He was working hard for his goal. He wanted to come first in the race, not a big goal but it mattered to him.
He crossed the boy in the second position and was two steps away from first. I loved watching him run and break his limits. It motivated me to work hard at my job. Today was no different; he was breaking his limits, I knew he would win, I wanted him to win. I jumped, cheered and clapped for the boy. He didn't seem to hear it, he was focused on his goal. Before he could cross the boy, he sprained his ankle, crashed shoulder-first on the ground and rounded twice before coming to hold.

I was stunned, this is not how it should end, this was unfair to the hard work he did, I could only think about this at the time. Racer crossed him one by one, he rose up to his feet not giving up. He tried to run but he fell back again, his shirt was filled with dust. He wasn't even able to finish the race. I couldn't wait any longer so I ran down the stands to him. To my surprise, he was smiling as he checked his ankle. I couldn't stop myself from asking for what reason he was smiling. The words that boy said to me that day hadn't left my mind ever since.
"I won, sir." He said, the smile never left his face.
"No boy, I am sorry but you lost." I bombed him with reality with a heavy heart. I filled me up with anger that some who

deserved to win had just lost. I was the same with me no matter how hard I worked I didn't get the credit.
"No, sir." He said and looked in my eyes and continued, "I won from myself. I beat my last year record, I'll work harder and then these types of things won't stop me from running." He pointed at his sprained ankle.
I was left speechless from what he had said. He was still positive even after he had lost not because of his mistake. He was looking forward to the next time. I just hugged the boy. That day a boy had taught me a big life lesson.

Japneet Chandoak

Japneet is a student studying in 9th grade in Vivek High School, Chandigarh. She is a teenager who loves to spend her free time reading and also writing.

For her, literature is a way to escape from the ordinary and stressful life into the bliss and peacefulness that literature seems to bring. This is the first time her works are being published in a book and she hopes much more will follow.

INSTA: @whatif.xx

Uncertainty

I've been thinking for too long,
Trying for so long.
Nothing seems to work,
Kinda have the feeling nothing can ever really work.

What do I really need?
Love?
A miracle for happiness?
Hope?

I'm still searching the answers for these questions,
Something I'd probably never find.
But for all it's worth,
I'd like to know.
Escaping reality never seemed more tempting,
Drowning myself in tears never felt so right.
Leaving behind the question for me of who am I?

Making mistakes is alright,
Having regrets is fine.
It's just a constant reminder of what's not right.
Drowning myself in who I used to be and who I want to be,
I lock myself in a maze.
Waiting for yet another miracle,
To save me from this undying uncertainty.

I got everything I wanted,
Yet, I can't help but feel the same.
Maybe all I need is to feel alive
And shield myself from my imaginary pain.

Friendly Dark

There's a part of me that used to haunt me,
It was the key to all the pain I'd ever faced and a painful reminder that the worst isn't over,
It never really is.

Teasing me with every bit of agony it could,
I let it drown me in the sea of misery,
Falling in and losing hope of all that was yet to be.

The darkness took over,
Feeling its way through the light that surrounded me.

But now, it's not scary anymore.
It's a part of me I don't run from,
A part of me that'll last for evermore.

It weird how safe it feels now,
How instead of scarring me,
It heals within.

When the friendly dark takes over,
I gently sink into the familiar sense of blind around me.

It's not how bad as it seems to be,
You can't run from who you are deep within and the friendly dark just seems to remind me

Foolish Wishes

In the forest where the birds chirp by,
I stare longingly at their smiles.
Jealously crawls its way in,
And I try to send it miles away.

I see it flow away,
Down the hills it goes and I wish it would never return.
But I've been wishing for things I can't have,
I've been wishing too long that it drives me mad.

Still I wish for it to go,
And take with it all the pain within.
But it flows too deep to ever not bother me again.

Sighing I make my way,
Away from the constant ache.
Again it's another foolish wish,
Something that could never be true again.
It's a sad world,
I realise.
And what's sadder is how we make it so,
Smiles don't hurt but pain does.
But all we want to do is feel the pain.

It's our choices that make us who we are,
We can choose to be happy or be sad.
It's all within.
Still I choose the pain,
At least it's better than all the fake happiness and the constant feign

Blinding Lights

Deep in thought,
I wondered what was left to be.
How far was I and how far was left to go.

Somethings are known and some don't,
Somethings are better left unsaid and some told.

What would be this though?
A tale to tell or a lie to hide?
Something to share or something to leave aside?

It could be both for all we know,
But the scars go deeper than the memories told.

Forgetting could be easy but forgiveness harder,
For the climb is always high without a ladder.

It all goes deep within,
Where remembering you is a sin,
And all the lights go dim.

It all comes to me,
How much is left to be.
The quantity of it haunts me in my dreams,
The truth comes as blinding lights,
Into everything I see.

Nothing Left To Say

I've spoken all the words I wanted you to say,
But some things are better left unsaid.
Some chapters better left unread.

You don't feel the same or maybe I've never felt this way,
Either way it's drowning me and nothing will ever be the same.

But it's worth a shot if something remains,
If our something's still there then maybe we can be okay.

I feel like you should say something,
Anything really.

But I guess after all,
There's nothing left to say.

Sushmita Singh

Sushmita Singh is a student pursuing Bachelors in Dental Surgery from School of Dental Sciences, Sharda University.She is in love with literature and arts. For her writing is a way of letting her emotions flow through her quill. As a co-author, this is her first venture.
INSTA: @sushmita_s7664

Prem Ki Yaatraa

Maine baarish ki motiyon main tumhara naam piro diya hai. Ab ye 46ahan v jayengi, kirtan karengi tumhare naam ka, Yugon- Yugon tak. Sayad kisi behte jharne ke paani main mere pukaar ke swar sun paao tum. Ya phir nadi ke behte paani ki kal kalahat main tumhe naam sunaayi de apna.

Ya phir ye baarish ki bundein aaj se kuch mahine, saalon, ya sadiyon baad mil jaayen samandar ke paani se, to fir uski lehrein har puranmaasi ki raat ko gayengi geet hamare Preet ka, us nispaap, nishchal prem ka jo Maine puri shradhaa se sirf tumse kiya hai.

Par yadi ek din dharti ke andar sama gyi ye jal ki bundein, aur kisi roz pyaas se vyaakul ho tum nalke se paani piyo, to us din tumhaare hothon ka sparsh paakar inhe moksh mil jaayega. Dheemi awaaz main anant baar kahi gyi prarthna ko uske araadhy mil jaayenge…

Demons and Angels

Thin threads
All loose and tangled
Darkness and light
Embracing each other
My demons and angels
A tug of war
That's what you'll find
If I break down my walls
Collect the stones
And make a staircase for you
A staircase that won't lead you inside my head
But only let you take a peek
Tell me, will you try to untangle my thoughts
Trying to save me?
Or will you look closely
And understand
That the web it creates
Prevents me from falling down.
Tell me, will you try to pull apart my day and night?
Just cause you love the sun but
Can't comprehend the moonlight?
Or will you look closely
And understand
That in the centre of their embrace
Lies the sunset
My chaotic but calm abode
Where I lie
And find peace.
Tell me, will you try to cut the rope
And drive my demons away?
Will you try to aid my angels in
Winning the battles ahead?

Or will you look closely
And understand
That you are an outsider and it's their home
That both the good and evil are my own.
That I am a sacred sin,
And they make me who I am.
Their constant war reminds me that I am not dead.
They remind me that being better is a choice
And I am the only one that I should dread.
I'll be lost without them
They are my guides
Cause they remind me of the paths
I'll never walk again.
They've taught me acceptance
And the fact that making mistakes is what
Makes us human.
So now let me tell you a secret that
Never try changing me,
Cause my demons and angels make a really good team,
When it comes to defending me.

Wisdom

Do wounds ever heal?
Do the desires ever die out?
I don't think so.
Somewhere beneath the skin,
Below the scars,
The wounds still bleed.
Somewhere beneath those closed eyelids,
In the infinite darkness,
The desires still live.
I guess, we just get too numb to feel the pain,
Go too far away to ever turn back again,
We all are graveyards
With a tree of life over every grave,
Roots feeding on tears and poison,
Fruits dripping with elixir,
Branches all carved and engraved.
Shaped by the axe of time,
Pruned by wisdom we stand tall,
It's all about learning and accepting,
That we're everything as well as nothing at all.

Mujhse Moh Nahi Hoga

Mujhse moh nhi hoga
Main nirmohi hoon,
Mujhse moh nhi hoga.
Main viyog main tumhaare ashru nhi bahaaungi
Naa Milan hone pe shringaar rachaaungi.
Jo jaana chahoge kahin tum to rokungi nhi tumhe,
Main swayam bairaagi hoon,
Raahi hoon,
Beshudh kahin door nikal jaaungi.
Mera koi gantavya nhi hoga
Kyunki main nirmohi hoon
Mujhse moh nhi hoga.
Main aatmiyata ki baatein karungi tumse,
Varsha ki siyaahi se
Chandrama ke prishth par likhi kavitaayein sunaungi tumhe.
Jaise kisi yogi ki jaap maala main rudraksh piroye jaate hain
Theek waise hi apne sabdon ke alankaar main piroungi
tumhe.
Main prem awasya karungi tumse ,
Parantu nashwar sarir ka khel
Mujhse nhi hoga.
Kyunki main nirmohi hoon,
Mujhse moh nhi hoga.
Yadi kabhi virakt vimukh ho jaaun vichlit ho is sansaar se,
To dhoondna kisi Himalay ke ghane wan main mujhe
Dhairya ki sugandh odhe baith na Samip tum
Tumhe drishya dikhaaungi anant brahmaand ka sajal nayan
main mere.
Main saath nibhaaungi awasya tumhara,
Kintu sadev saath rehne ka pran mujhse nhi hoga,
Kyunki main nirmohi hoon
Mujhse moh nhi hoga.

Samridhi Jairath

Samridhi was born on August 07 in a family of working class people, with a defence background in Chandigarh, India. From her very childhood, she was hesitant to express herself. It was only in the year 2020 when the whole world was caged in their homes due to threat of corona virus that she decided to free her thoughts by giving words to her feelings & cutting down the barriers with the world. She started up with a writing page on Instagram named @pinpricks_of_life & aims to grow better each day. For she believes the world is not what the eyes see, but what the mind interprets it to be.

INSTA: @pinpricks_of_life

Why There Is So Much Pain?

Hatred & greed have become an unstoppable rain,
Causing the mindfulness to drain.
Why there is so much pain?
Evils remain unnamed,
Vitality of youth gone in vain,
Humanity pushed into the mindless game of fame,
Oh it's such a shame,
Then we say our perceptions aren't to be blamed,
Oh it's such a shame.

What Is Sorrow?

The pain left unborrowed or the memories which refuse to unfollow?
The voice which was swallowed or the echoes that follow,
Trust me it's never too late to bury them deep in a hollow,
It's never too late to start it all over again,
Let your doubts & sadness drain,
It's never too late to start it all over again.

(1)

Maybe a few things are meant to be dealt alone,
It's you who has to earn your own throne.
It's not the people who were at fault,
Nor you the one who trusts a lot.
It's not your heart which was played,
Nor the emotions cut with a blade,
Let it go like a boulevard of broken
morning dreams,
Let it all go down the stream.
Let's not see the pain in the journey
but the strength which brought
you all the gain.

(2)

There are times when your eyes are sore,
Was it the memos of the promises that were torn,
Or the unfulfilled hopes that were born?

(3)

There are times when your doubts roar,
And Set your consciousness offshore,
But, don't forget that you too are worth something more.

(4)

At times it’s okay to take short breaks from all the aches,
Cause the better you deserves to be at peace,
Not stuck & seized.

(5)

Memories would shade,
People would fade,
It’s what you really felt in your heart would stay
Choice is yours to sit back & lay,
Or to live in the new day.

(6)

Life’s better when you start knowing the blessings you have gained,
Rather than pushing yourself to revisit the same lanes and
Feeling the same old pain,
All over & over again.

Sarisha Singh

Sarisha Singh was born on March 2nd in a family of easy going people, her mother being a lecturer and her father being a senior advocate. She is currently in 10th grade in Carmel Convent School, Chandigarh. She is a writer here, and strangely, the owner of a blog. It was her lifelong dream to be a blogger and make people aware of the current situations that are going on, in various parts of the world. But, unfortunately she couldn't do so due to the COVID-19 crisis. Now she is the youngest writer anyone has seen and her writings are spectacular. This became possible when she had ample time in her hands to do something creative and innovative. This surely has helped her and the people around her.

She started up with a writing blog on WordPress, the address being www.allaboutlifecomonline.wordpress.com and is currently quite active having views and comments from people living in countries like: Ethiopia, Romania and The Philippines. She also believes that it is her solemn duty to make people sitting in different parts of the world aware of the current situations.

Don't Judge a Book by its Movie

You've guessed it rightly. In this blog, I will be talking about why books are better than movies. Ever since the first book was adapted into a movie ("Sherlock Holmes Baffled" in 1900, if you're wondering), there has been much discussion about which is better– Reading the original book or watching the movie adaptation? You've heard it a thousand times before: The book is better than the movie. Is this just some people's way of seeming intellectually superior? Or is there something to it? Let's talk about the book vs movie argument. Each version has its own merits, which is probably why the debate has never been laid to rest, but to me there is a clear winner. As an ardent book reader and lover (and hopefully a future writer) I will always side with the book– no matter how good the movie that follows may or may not be. But sometimes, a great director with a vision gets the film just right. I never liked a film version of the Romeo and Juliet until Baz Luhrmann brought it to the big screen. Here are the reasons why….

Books allow you to know what the characters are actually thinking.

One of my top arguments for why I will always prefer books is that books actually allow you to know what the characters are thinking or feeling. In movies, you have to rely on two things: 1) a character telling you what they (or others) are thinking or feeling, or 2) the subtext you can pick up from the performance of the actor. This may be fine for the people who pay attention that closely, but it is a lot more difficult if you're someone like me. There are also certain thoughts or feelings that you can't tell just by looking at an actor. Take a heart pounding faster, for example.

Books allow you to get to know the characters better.

As a result of many of the reasons on this list, books let you get to know the characters better. You get to know their actual thoughts (like I said in #1), you spend more time with them, and you learn more details about them. Take the Harry Potter series– one of the most famous book to movie adaptations–for example. If you just watch the movies without reading the books, there is a lot that you don't know about the characters because it was left out of the movie. This brings me to my next reason.

Books don't have to cram everything into a two-hour time frame.

Books get to tell their stories in hundreds (sometimes thousands) of pages that take hours to read. A movie has a limited time frame of roughly two hours. You know, that is unless you divide the story into two movies like they have been doing. Because of this, important events and details often get left out of the movie in order to fit the limited time frame and/or because they may or may not work well with the medium. If you just watch the movie, you aren't really getting the whole story–just the condensed version.

Books are more detailed.

There are certain things you can do in a book that you just can't in a movie. Besides letting you know the characters' thoughts, which I've already touched on, books also let you in on more basic story and plot details. It is a lot easier to set up the story and explain what is going on in a book simply because of the medium/format. An author can use anywhere from a line of dialogue to a paragraph to even a whole chapter to give the readers the background information they need. Movies have fewer options to do this and mostly have to rely on dialogue to get the job done. It takes a good balance to make this work.

Books allow you to experience the story as the author intended it.

Another one of the reasons that I am most passionate about is that books allow you to experience everything as the author intended it to be (for the most part). There are no big Hollywood agendas or studio/director/screenwriter changes made to the story when you're reading the book. The publishing company, yes, but not Hollywood. I can tell you that there is nothing more disappointing for a book lover than seeing one of your favorite stories be butchered and changed when it is made into a movie. My fellow Percy Jackson fans will know what I am talking about.

Books can stay with you forever.

There's not really much I can add to this one other than the books that we read and love, whether as a child or an adult, have a way of sticking with us and influencing us in ways we could never have imagined. The aforementioned Harry Potter series does this for me. Even though I read these books at a very young age, the stories have stuck with me to this day and remain one of my all-time favorites.

It's clear to see that I have a lot of opinions when it comes to this particular topic. I love movies just as much as the next person, but when it comes to book-to-movie adaptations, there really is no contest for me. Because no matter how great the visuals and effects for a movie may be, nothing will ever beat it's more detailed, intimate, imaginative, and character-driven book. Anyone who disagrees can leave me a comment so we can respectfully discuss it.

We are Raising a Generation of Spoiled Kids or Brats

I know this topic sounds a little absurd but nowadays a lot of parents that I know and may not even know are raising spoiled kids or as commonly known as brats. This generation has turned out to be full of spoiled kids who regularly throw tantrums whenever they want something. They just don't know the meaning of the word "NO".

If we compare the kids from the last generation to the kids from this generation, we find that the kids from last generation were much disciplined compared to the current scenario. Let's see how........ Fifty years ago, if you didn't follow the rules at school, you would probably get corporal punishment. Teachers were a figure of authority. They expected the best behaviour from you. Doing your best was important. Every day there was an assembly where you were asked to be strong, take part in school activities, respect the school, and respect the teachers. You had to wear a uniform—no exceptions. If you said something, you would be sent home and not allowed to return until you wore the prescribed clothes. This was how kids behaved at school.

At home, it was possible that you could get scolded for being disrespectful or not following "house rules." You could be grounded for not applying yourself at school. A similar thing could happen you if you stayed out late or annoyed the neighbours. Responsibility was important. Children were told what their responsibilities were. Letting someone down was serious. Children were free to play outside if there was daylight and they stayed in earshot of mum who would call your name when it was time to be indoors.

But nowadays,

I am glad that some of those things no longer take place in school or, overall, at home. Corporal punishment has no place in our society. There are far more effective ways of disciplining children than beating them. Teachers are not so strict figures anymore. They are much closer to children. Emphasis is put on the causes of bad behaviour rather than just managing it. At a supermarket, your 10-year-old demands that you buy him a box of chocolates. When you refuse, he throws a tantrum and since you don't want to create a scene in front of him, you give it to him and your son goes home happier. Well, surely, most parents must have come across such a situation at least once in their life. However, have you ever thought of the number of times you've given in to your kid's demands? Chances are that it's more than often and you might be raising a spoilt child. No one wants to raise a spoiled kid. But would you know one if you had one? By grandparents' definition, all of today's children — with their Disney videos, wardrobe full of branded clothes, and weird types of classes — could be considered spoiled.

So who's at fault?

It is more parents' faulty upbringing of the kid that leads him/her to be spoilt. The earlier generation of parents was more relaxed and had more time for their kids. However, with most parents working today, they don't spend enough time with their kids, so they make up by giving in to their demands and as a result, the child is spoilt. Also, a few parents have an experience of previous generations, and for the most part that's good.

But sometimes in the effort to be kinder, gentler parents, moms and dads let their sweet little darlings get spoilt. Some parents put up with truly awful behavior. If your 20-month-old has never heard the word *no*, for instance, how will she handle hearing it when she's 13 and wants to get her nose pierced?

Unspoiling your child

Parents should set consistent limits and toddlers who have clear boundaries feel secure and are less likely to act out with bratty behavior. With a toddler, it's best to stick with just three or four simple and less overburdening rules, like "No hitting," "Don't interrupt adults," and "Pick up your toys," because too many orders can overwhelm kids and adults. If your child throws a tantrum when he/she doesn't get his way, try to ignore the crying until it's over. Once your child learns that he won't get the desired attention, he'll be less likely to repeat it. Saying these words may even make your child more cooperative "I love you and I'm sorry you're mad, but I'm not giving in and you can't hit or throw things when you don't get your favourite things." It also helps to lessen his feelings of frustration. Saying something like, "I know it's really hard to stop playing but it's time to go home," also helps at times.

It may be tough to resist spoiling now, but the result will be huge. Your child will learn how to manage feelings, cooperate, follow rules, and have self-control. These lessons will be beneficial throughout your child's life. So don't let your kids turn into spoiled brats. Start saying "NO" to them as soon as they start to understand words.

Chandni Sachdeva

Chandni Sachdeva is a human resource by profession. She is living a confused and ironical life in the city of New Delhi. She loves day dreaming and might run away in a circus someday. She loves travelling and writes sometimes.
INSTA: chandni_sachdeva

The Lost Footsteps

Get up! It's 5:30 a.m. Else, we'll get late
for the walk". Everyday my morning used to start with these words falling on my ears. My grandfather used to call me and wake me up. He used to keep shouting my name until I got off the bed. I was 14 and there was hardly any day when I was spared of this. He made sure that I brushed my teeth and wore my sports shoes before leaving the house. Usually, I used to be half asleep on my way to the park.

Daily, as we stepped out of the house, my first view used to be of an aged rag-picker, collecting bits of garbage and rotten materials thrown by nearby people and putting them inside a huge bag on his hunched back. The old man had a fringe of grey-white hair around his balding, mottled scalp. He had a wizened face and it was pretty obvious that his creaky bones labored hard to bring about every small movement of his. He had the resigned look of one who knows that at his age life had stopped giving and started taking. He was very aged, feeble and had a very loose skin. He wore torn clothes and was very thin. But whenever I used to look at his eyes, it always had many untold stories in it. Yes!! His eyes said something. A story that he wanted to tell, but could find no willing listener. He would be about 70 years, near about my grandfather's age. And like my grandfather's routine, he too used to be there at 6:00 a.m. regularly without failure. Not a single morning passed when we missed seeing him at his work.

He greeted us with a gracious smile which expressed his delight upon seeing us. While returning from our walking session, my grandfather would buy him a cup of tea and a packet of biscuits. His eyes used to light up with pleasure the moment he used to get these. He used to sit on the nearby bench regularly and have them. And this was a routine which was being followed for almost three years now.

Then one day, we did not see him. And that one day became a week and then another week. Initially, we thought that the old man would have fallen ill and hence not appearing. As the days passed, this disappearance strangely turned into a genuine cause for concern for my grandfather. He kept asking fellow morning walkers for some possible information regarding the whereabouts of this old rag-picker. But nobody knew anything; in fact although regulars to the park, many had never noticed the wretched old fellow going about doing his daily job. By the end of the second week, my grandfather frankly admitted that he intended to find out something-anything- about this lone rag-picker but just couldn't figure out where he would start from.
Each morning, my grandfather would sit on the bench, hitherto, reserved by the rag-picker and gaze around, as if scanning the surroundings for a glimpse of the familiar old face. Actually, he would try to think of ways to start his search. Although, I felt that my grandfather was being a bit too sentimental about that rag-picker and expressed as much to him, my grandfather would only retort that a person who was a regular sight for three whole years just could not vanish into thin air. Suddenly, one day, my grandfather came up with this idea of approaching the security guard of a house adjacent to the park. Chances were that the guard would have noticed this daily rag-picker and knew something about him. As luck would have it, grandfather did ask the guard and the guard certainly knew about this rag-picker. And what he narrated was nothing close to what we were expecting.

The old man was a resident of a house in the next neighborhood and our narrator's uncle happened to be the watchman of an apartment adjacent to his house. Some years back, soon after the demise of his ailing wife, his son sent him to an old age home, in order to relocate overseas with his wife and child. The house was put up on rent, a fact that was hidden from the old man.

The old man could not adjust at the old-age home, but upon returning to his house, realized that it was occupied by tenants who had not met him and were not aware of his existence. Grief-stricken, he roamed about the neighborhood aimlessly for the whole day. A nearby bakery store offered him some muffins and upon hearing his plight, suggested that he seek shelter at a nearby pavement dwellers' night-shelter. At the night-shelter, the old man came upon various job prospects from fellow pavement dwellers and decided that the profile of the rag-picker would best fit him. The rag-pickers could sell the garbage collected from roads on a daily basis.

Thus, every morning he used to visit streets and collect the garbage and bits of trash and used to sell them to earn a meal for him-self.

The narrator's watchman uncle, having witnessed the old man's transition from a gentleman to a rag-picker, had expressed his anguish to the narrator. How could educated people behave in such an unimaginable manner? Unable to help in any substantial manner, this watchman uncle would meet him at times to pass on some food and spare clothes. Such times, he would actually express his opinions to the old man.

Amazingly, the old man did not blame his son for his plight. To him, his son was rightfully ambitious to seek better job prospects elsewhere; putting his aged father in an old-age home was a practical and wise decision because there were skillful attendants and same-age group people to give company; renting out the house was also a wise way to maintain it; how could an old man be expected to take care of a house and stay all alone?

Rather, it was he who could not adjust himself at the old age home, hence had left it. In fact, had he shown enough courage

to either accompany them overseas or stay back in his own house, possibly his son wouldn't have decided to send him to an old age home. He had not wanted to inform his son about his flight from the old age home as that would land his son in a dilemma – whether to quit overseas prospects or to stay put there. He had a strong belief that his son would leave all to be at his side, but as a father, where he could not provide better opportunities to his son, he had no right to snatch away the prevailing good life from him.

While collecting garbage a few weeks ago, he had contracted some infection that led to his demise two weeks back. In death also, he showed amazing far-sight. Apparently, when his sickness from the infection had intensified, he had contacted the old age home and convinced them to collect him from the night shelter. This was to ensure that he passed away within the walls of the old-age home and keep his son blissfully unaware of the rag-picking days.

Although a bratty teenager with no worldly care, I could still feel the pain upon hearing the old man's story. My grandfather stood still for quite some time, staring at the pavement, then slowly turned and walked back to the park bench and sat there. "How does it feel to sleep on the floor?" He wondered aloud. "Maybe not any different than sleeping on the bed! After all, sleep is what matters when you are tired; 'where to sleep' becomes immaterial then." I kept quiet while I watched anxiously at my pensive grandfather.

He sat for some more time, then went to the tea vendor and made his usual purchase of tea and biscuits. He pointed out some wild flowers growing out of the bushes near the park boundary wall, for me to pluck. We returned to the park-bench and placed the tea and biscuit packet on one corner of the bench and placed the flowers next to these. We bowed our heads and, am sure, my grandfather's prayer matched mine when I prayed 'Rest in peace old man'.

From the next morning inwards, we always left tea and biscuits on the same park bench. It didn't matter who had them. What was important that, daily, these would have probably brought a joyous smile on some poor soul's face. We also changed our morning walk path to match the path taken by the rag-picker as if to retrace 'His lost footsteps' as a tribute to this unique personality.

Love!

Chandni

Jasnoor Arora

Jasnoor Arora is an undergraduate student in the field of Biotechnology at GGDSD College, Chandigarh. She became a book lover as they help her to acquire a unique perspective towards her surroundings. She finds literature as a way to comfort herself. She considers herself as not a passionate writer but thinks of literature as a source to express her unspoken thoughts. Her writings are based on the feelings she has experienced in life. As a co-author, this is her debut. She hopes that people will find her writings relatable and soothing. She feels that the only way she knows to express herself precisely is when she pens it down.
INSTA: @nooruuuu_

Fathom

The day I slept,
Was the day I lost.
The day I woke up,
Was the day I regretted.

The Sun was here,
Wind blew cool.
The day was here,
And here, I stood still.

It was the day I went alive.
I went alive and realised,
That I may have lost many,
But gained much.

Much more than I ever expected !

Perception

I don't regret no more,
As the feeling was surreal.
For me love is no bore,
Since the moment made me squeal.

I was never your choice,
For you I was just a collectible.
Still you didn't seem to rejoice,
And now I feel a little skeptical.

I became uptight,
Because I felt insecure.
Now, I want to set it right,
For it is the only cure.

I never tried to bluff,
Nor to make it tough.
You made me feel handcuffed,
And now I have had enough.

Lovelorn

To have you as my crush,
Was no less than a four flush.
I wait for you just in case,
But next to me is an empty space.

Even though I knew,
We were not meant to be.
I still want to be with you,
Not in dreams but in reality.

Suddenly I woke up to Actuality,
With a bunch of tear-stained tissue.
Thinking while I drink my coffee,
And hoped it all to be untrue.

I wish it could be stopped,
But I still let it happen.
Now it's like my heart's been chopped,
And everything seems to be crashin'.

Azure

Layed down on my back reclining,
The world's upside down me sighting.

While soaking the sun in my lawn,
I let out a sleepy yawn.

Now I start to feel light-headed,
And go in for the sleep I never intended.

I imagine myself walking in the sky,
Sitting on a cloud to see the time fly.

Woke up to a setting sun,
The kids gather one by one.

Now the game has begun,
Let's play and have some fun.

Melancholy

Walking in the dark without an aim,
There's a storm in me alight.
Unsure about how to tame,
Scars healed by the moonlight.

I have people who do not care,
If I am sad or in despair.
Is it okay if I cry myself to sleep?
In a tender slumber, I still weep.

My words may be blunt,
But I did not intend to affront.
Surrounded but I still am lonely,
Now all they say I talk baloney.

I hope someone to see beyond the smile,
And feel the pain that I hide.
Tears flow as long as river Nile,
While I still am grinning wide.

Arshpreet Kaur Dharwal

It is both a curse and a blessing to feel everything so invincibly when you're a teenager just like me. I am just a simple girl who is perceived to be exceptionally difficult by many. Being a person who can easily absorb and feel, not only the happiness of others but also their pain and anguish is what inspired me to write, what I am going to call the first ever short story written by me in the future. This story is a crystalline depiction of who I am as a person and the only message that I would like to convey to its readers is that even though love hurts sometimes, never lose hope yet choose to become the love you never received and it will come back to you in unique ways.
INSTA: @arshpreet_dharwal

With All My Heart

Love is a surprise. It comes at the most unexpected times and knocks down your walls like no other thing in the world. Love redefines every single choice a person ever makes and suddenly makes you question everything. Love is powerful and being loved the right way fills everything with happiness. Such was the story of the beautiful Rose Dawson and handsome Jack Cunnings.

It was pouring down excessively that day, the aroma of freshly baked goods coming from the bakeries on every corner filled the streets of Midwood, a small neighborhood in Brooklyn. Despite the heavy rainfall, the people were still in their usual rush to get to their works. And in the middle of all this chaos, there was the beautiful Rose dressed in black clothes and rainy boots holding a white rose in one of her hand and an umbrella in the other. As usual, she was on her way to the Central Library to return the books she had rented earlier.

She was fond of reading, for her reading was a way of escaping from the cruel realities of the real world into a land of magic, fairies, dragons, and warriors.

"Gee! It's horrible outside today Mrs. Ray!" says Rose as she enters the library. Mrs. Ray was the head librarian of the Central Library. "Oh you poor thing, you're soaking wet" says Mrs. Ray as she offers her tissues the moment she sees Rose. Mrs. Ray was very fond of Rose and thought of her as a sweet girl which was why being of a quiet and arrogant nature, Rose was the only girl to whom Mrs. Ray ever spoke to nicely at the library. This is for "you Mrs. Ray" says Rose as she handles the beautiful white Rose to her.

Every day she brought a white Rose for Mrs. Ray as she grew them in her backyard.

"Have you got my book today?" Rose inquires, "Oh dear, you will not be disappointed today!" answers Mrs. Ray. "Go on and look at aisle 5 shelf 4, it just got in yesterday evening! And if you have trouble finding it, a new boy working in that aisle named Jack, ask him about it!" she adds.

She goes on to look for her book which she has been dying to read for days, but upon looking for it and unable to find it, she starts calling out for Jack as instructed by Mrs. Ray.

"Jack….Jack. Is Jack here?" she asks around.

"Hey there! Are you looking for me?" comes a voice from behind her and when she turns around, there he was, Jack! The new boy. Jack had hazel eyes, black hair, a fair complexion, and a smile that looked just as charming as a prince of a magical fairytale. The moment Rose turns and looks at him, she became speechless for a moment.

Whereas for Jack, Rose was the most beautiful girl he had ever seen. Luscious lips, golden hair and rosy cheeks did justice to her. It was love at first sight for both of them. Unexpected and unplanned.

"I'm looking for a book called Wuthering Heights" Rose asks nervously.

"Oh, I'll get it for you right away!" Jack answers.

"Here it is! It's my favorite book you know!" Jack tells Rose. It was the first time he engaged himself in a conversation with a stranger. That was the point, she did not seem strange to him at all.

"Mine as well!" Rose replied with a tone of surprise.

"I've been dying to get my hands on this for days now", Rose begins to tell. "It's a classic!" both of them add at the same time which leads to pleasant laughter between the two.

It was soon that both of them started talking and getting along with each other. They started meeting every day as Rose came to the library more often. It didn't take long for them to become friends which later turned into love, passionate, and undying love. They started going out to places and also met

each other's families. It was not so long before Jack proposed to Rose about marrying him and she says yes to him.

It was a match made in heaven!" the people said. Soon after the proposal, Jack was walking home one day, after work. Unaware of the fate that was ahead of him, while crossing the road, he suddenly faints in the middle of the crossing.

When he was taken into the hospital, he was unconscious, the hospital called Rose to tell her what had happened and as soon as she hears about it, it does not take her long to get there. When she meets the doctor, he moves her to his office to discuss Jack's case.

You might have to take a seat for this Rose." The doctor says.

"What is it, doctor? What is wrong with Jack?" she asks sitting down in his office.

It is with great pain that I have to inform you that Jack has a hole in his heart." The doctor says.

"His heart is compromised and he is in dire need of a heart transplant without it, he won't be able to survive." The doctor adds. "Jack only has a few days before his heart stops working".

This heart- crushing news drives Rose into a complete shock! The love of her life, her partner was about to die and she could not do anything about it. Soon she gathers herself and decides to spend every moment with Jack.

A few days pass and along with them, Jack's condition became worse. The doctor informs Rose that the hospital was unable to arrange a heart transplant so soon for Jack.

Finding out about this, Rose asks the doctors to prepare for Jack's surgery and tells them that she will arrange for his transplant soon. The doctor miraculously receives a heart for Jack's transplant the same evening. Jack's surgery goes well and his life was saved all thanks to Rose.

He wakes up after four days, on seeing his whole family there but not Rose, he asked about her, which when the looks on everyone's faces in the room who came to meet Jack fade.
"Where is Rose?" He asks his mother.
His mother with a crushing tone says, "Here son, it's a letter from dear Rose, she asked us to give this to you, the moment you woke up".
Jacks begins to read;

My love, your heart is getting weaker by the day, and the hospital is not able to arrange a donor for you. You gave me a forever in numbered days Jack. I love you with all my heart which is why I am giving it to you. I will live right beside you, breathe from inside you, and feel everything along with you. Find peace knowing that you have my heart now and that I will be right beside you every step of the way.

I love you. Your beloved Rose.

Jack's mother hand him a bouquet of white roses which Rose had made for him.
Jack starts crying and hugging Rose's roses.

Ishita Kaur

She is a second year student, pursuing English Literature with Psychology from SD College, Chandigarh. She is basically from Jharkhand. She has been writing since her 10th grade. She wishes to publish her work as a quotic book soon. She posts regularly on her page @scribbled_tales. She liked reading fiction so much that she didn't knew when she wanted to write them. She hopes you like her work. Happy Reading!
INSTA: @scribbled_tales

The Traffic Jam

Who in this whole world loves traffic at all? But the things that we don't like are supposed to take place again and again. Be it a heartbreak, or a favourite dish that you don't want to end. But it is good that things end. It makes us value things more. To take a lesson in life is important. Life teaches us lessons in some way or the other and that lesson is for good.

Vani was a quite chirpy girl around her friends. A complete extrovert for people she knew, and a complete stranger of mixed feelings for the people she was a stranger. She was a girl who was reserved with her chores and her feelings for the one who had left her a year ago. She was so true to her feelings that she imagined all the non-living scenarios with him in her everyday chores.

Vani who was a literature student in Chandigarh lived in a hostel with so much loved friends. It is strange how you leave your family to live in the hostel so far and then you create a very little family of friends who are so much worth.

Traffic in a city like Chandigarh is very calm. People treat everyone as they are total strangers to them. It is like you carry your own business while I do so too. Everybody is a total stranger to everybody. Yesterday, Vani was struck in this traffic jam. She was coming back from the terrace garden. The hostel timings were very strict and she had to return back to the hostel until 6:30. It was just 5 so it was no such hurry for her then. She was sitting inside her cab that had arrived a bit early with her head tilted to the glass window. She was making a snap to continue the streak with people she barely talked now.

It is so strange how you personally know very less people in your lives and then there are people whom you connect so better on the internet. The people whom you know in your real life have so much less of you than the people who you connect on social media. In real life you try portraying yourself in the best perfect way possible so that the person in front of you judges you to be a perfect one. But the people whom we connect with on the internet are far so much more understanding. There is no fear of being

judged on how much perfect you are, or either you do not have to worry about them to create assumptions about you.

This generation is so like that they just want peace of mind. Atleast some people do. But a coin always has two sides. There are people who also take away your peace when you want them is to be your peace for once and for all. But the destiny has so much to give you; more than you think and just much more than you expect or imagine it can. Life chicko, it is very very unpredictable with all the odds happening to you daily.

Out of all the odds that had ever happened to Vani in her entire lifetime, this traffic jam was going to be the most amazing one. Vani, who was just so engrossed in her internet world after sending the streak that her head was engrossed so low that it had started hurting now. She took her head up and turned her head left to feel relieved. She sat back straight and turned towards right side where she could see the jam clearly through the window of her cab. To her awe, Vani saw a number plate that was just so familiar to her.

It was a car, not so far from her cab; not so far from her sight. The number plate was more familiar to her than the car would ever be. To find a number plate with JH engraved with it was just so odd, for very less people; more specifically very less students go to Chandigarh for their further studies. The scenarios in which everything had ended a year ago all came hovering to her mind within a very short span of time. It was like she was took a back after moving on for good now. Move-on was it? Or was it just a show for the people around her so that they believe her words that she was happy. Only she knew how she had suffered all this long and how difficult was it for her. To tell people that she was happy when she wasn't. To cry out loud in those nights when she was made sleep alone in that hostel room. To give up on food when she was made to eat forcefully. And to end her life which she was living forcefully. In no time Vani knew who it was inside the car that had JH number plate. His smiling face hovered her mind like it had never left her. And if speaking truly, it had indeed been engraved to her mind; to her heart. Her heart had started pounding fast. She could hear how fast her breathing had turned. If she would have been with any of her friends', they would have never allowed her do what she was thinking. It had turned out a good idea of her best friend from hostel to let her go alone to somewhere quiet. She was alone in the cab and all she thought was to get off the cab and run to him. Run to him to embrace him and own him like never.

Breakups you know, they have grown so much common in this generation. It was so good in the old times when parents decided the life partners of their children when it was a right time for them. They were married for good and there was no scope of a breakup.

Speaking of a time ahead when our parents were young, it was good back then for them because they valued relationships and commitments; rather than this generation who takes relationships and commitments for just a mere time pass.

Vani had a complete black out from the reality in that very moment. The past haunted her like it always did and the thought that this chance of visiting him had come after a very long span of time hovered all over her mind. She was frozen and all she could do was nothing. She just sat back in her seat and froze for a while. For a while that traffic jam didn't seem real. For a moment that face to her didn't seem real. For a moment she couldn't just believe in her eyes that she was seeing him after whole of a year. Their breakup was a world turning event for both Vani and Mihir. One wanted to express her feelings out of her heart so bad, but had no ways to contact him and Mihir had digested the fact that they were separated for good. This is what Vani had believed for this whole year. But now that she had her time to face him; to go to him and tell about her feelings, she was froze. They both had a mutual feeling for one another but they

knew they couldn't do anything but accept the fate. Atleast this is what Vani has been doing all along her life.
Mihir's face on a late evening gave her a soothing time with herself. His pictures had filled his space all this time and she finally had her time to just wait and stare at him for a while. She just couldn't understand anything. She always had imagined how she would react when she would see him from nowhere, but everything went to vain. She had wanted to meet Mihir for so long, but she had no courage to ask him so.

There were thoughts on her mind after seeing his face after the entire year now when the red light turned green. This time for her fleeted so quick that she couldn't understand why her cab had started moving and that Mihir's car had also ignited. In no time when she realized that the red lights had turned green, she dialed Mihir's number and in no time she could hear the caller tune in his number. "Baby I'm dancing in the dark, with you between my arms. Barefoot on the grass listening to our favourite song. When you said you looked a mess, I whispered underneath my breath." And trying that he received the phone call. For a moment she could do nothing but breathe over the call when Mihir ended the silence and said his first word to her since this year. Hello! He said over the call. Vani was just so took aback by Mihir's voice. To listen to his voice notes and call recordings and to hear his voice to back normal again, was a complete treat to her ears. That soothing voice hadn't changed since then. She cut the silence that her thoughts had created after his hello! And thinking nothing over what she was going to speak now, she said that she had seen him in the road where his car had stopped and he didn't know for a moment what Vani was talking about.
She explained him about what she was saying and Mihir told her to stop wherever she could and wait for him. She asked the driver of the cab to stop somewhere close and paid him. In her mind somewhere she was aware of the hostel curfew, but what mattered to her more was just meeting him after an entire year.

She stood there and within a minute her phone flashed his name with the incoming call. Mihir asked where she was and reached her within half a minute. She hopped into the front seat just like the old times without a thought. She settled in and tied her seat belt. Both were silent for a while. Mihir reversed the car and took it somewhere close to her hostel in an eluded place. She was happy in her mind that he still remembered the timings of her hostel.

After he stopped his car, both Vani and Mihir were silent. Vani couldn't compose herself and she started to cry. Mihir held her hand, wiped her tears and kissed her forehead. They were holding hands after a long year. Vani placed her head on Mihir's shoulder and Mihir couldn't just compose his happiness. It was visible that not only Vani but also Mihir had wanted this to happen. Mihir and Vani were both on the same page who wanted to make things normal back again like before. Their love had once again united and they were with each other again for good.

It's simple how you love someone so truly that you don't think for another moment whether it is right or wrong to move back to them. But just remember whatever you do in that heat of the moment is what you have been waiting to do since long. So never regret on something that you did somewhere in your life in that heat of the moment. They are just a call away and you can just simply dial their number to express your feeling to them before it is too late.

M. Shalini Mary

Shalini Mary. M is from Tamil Nadu, who is a student pursuing English Literature from St. Anne's Arts and Science College, Chennai. She took literature as a choice, but eventually it became her voice. She is a confessional writer. As a budding writer this is a great opportunity for her to bloom bright. This is her first endeavour as a writer. And she is very grateful for this fortuitous moment to write with other co-authors.

INSTA: @_unknown_words_

Life With Depression

"Every time I searched for a way
It hunted me like a prey
I never knew it'll stay
Slowly my life became grey"

"When I look into the mirror I can see myself
Beautiful breaking down,
Gracefully tearing apart and hopefully smiling that
One day everything will come to an end"

"It's true that we can't be truthful to everyone,
But let's try to be truthful to the ones in the mirror"

"Even the scare can decorate your life beautiful
So, everyone has a scare which makes them beautiful.
Be beautiful in your own way!"

Perfect

"Not being perfect for
Ourselves is just perfect than
Being perfect for others..."
"Don't let your miserable life to ruin your dreams".

"Maturity is when we realize that the virginity is just
The status of youth!"
"In the process of making the "Better Me", I just
Realized that I lost the "Real Me".

Hostage

In a room with no windows and lights
Who knows when its dawns or twilights
This unpredictable soreness which I adore

That grew up from the road I travelled before.
Cuffs and Chains are not a concern at all;
Compared to the past trauma which,

"I don't want to recall!"
Emotions are engraved on these bricky walls
Where my season became forever fall
I left my mind to rot in mortifying vain,
There lays my heart resting with this stinging pain
But there's a reason why I stay after all
Because I know I'm a hostage of my soul.

She

She was born with grudges in her fate
In the world which filled with hate,
Then still she had the hope to survive
As she knows that is her last revive.
She is a beautiful piece of art;
Which made all her dreams tear apart
She was jailed in her own house
Where she hid all her feelings behind the cloud.
She dreamed high beyond the stars
But this society made her to sit behind the walls
Yet she is a silent warrior with a task
Who is being obliged to hide all her
Insecurities with a mask!

Dhruv Kapoor

Dhruv has always been someone who is enthusiastic and will try his best at whatever he puts his mind to, he was born in Chandigarh, to a working class family, and one thing he's very determined about, is improving, with everything single day and thing he does. He likes art, poetry, photography and is a tech geek too. He began writing recently, in 2020, the circumstances switched all of a sudden, and writing seemed to be the best release, he now writes at @dkx1611 and his other account, @ateen_ager where he posts his work along with his clicks.

INSTA: @dkx1611

A Losing Battle

I can fight it ,
but can I win?
I can feel it,
my chest cracking open,
the voices egtting louder and louder,
heart pacing,
eyes tearing up,
I try turning the music,
the pit in my stomach deepens,
my mouth open but ,
no sounds arise from the hollow of my
dry choked throat,
the fear and shock kicks in,
as I sink into billions of thoughts at the same time,
its useless fighting it isn't it,
eventually I fall into the never ending abyss,
darkness surrounding me,
unable to breathe, and contemplate,
hoping its the last time but it never is

The Escapism Through Music

Oh, the soothing chords of the acoustic,
The beats which are not just beats,
But vibrations of my soul,
Don't I just love music?
And how it makes me feel at my peak?
How it makes me feel free to do anything,
To sing,
To dance,
To jump,
To twirl,
To swivel,
And sometimes even fall down to the floor,
I AM FREE TO BE MYSELF,
Is all I hear in every lyric, in every sound,
Everything is in place,
Once those two pieces of plastic are
In the grooves of my ears,
Every lyric relatable,
Every sound hitting the soul hard,
It's Elixir to the mouth,
The Mona Lisa to the eyes,
The softest and most relaxing
Sensation to the touch,
It carries me to another world,
Where everything is perfect,
MUSIC IS AN ESCAPE

The Phoenix

Oh, you fallen Beauty
Broken, into pieces,
Shared unto others
Lonely at the bottom of the dark pit you lay,
Melancholic as it is,
You fail to see one thing, love
That there's only one way you can go,
UP, FLYING STRAIGHT UP,
Unfurl your gorgeous wings,
The fire inside you fueling your flight,
But you MUST GET UP,
Stir away from this dejection,
Rise from your ashes,
And set this gloom ablaze,
After all to shine,
Don't you have to burn first?

The Great Escape

Plink! Plink!
Fell the drops of blood
Knife in his hand,
Drops being formed on the other wrist,
Death slowing pushing the life out of him,
Silently taking his heart for some last laps,
Stealthily making his eyes flutter,
The blood lit flame beneath him,
A vessel to satisfy the devil's bloodlust,
His body feeling the pain quietly,
His soul died screaming for help,
Legs going numb, Thud! On the floor he lay,
Family rushing but the door locked,
He smiles as death takes over him,
His last breath,
A sigh of relief for it was not painful at all,
For him it was the final and only way,
For him it was ecstasy.

Beauty In The Madness

Her smile resembles the devil's she’s a soul that'll possess you
Her voice never leaves your ears,
Her actions have consequences,
She reels you in with her mystical black eyes
And you are forever intoxicated by her existence
She is a scar that never fades,
One sleight of her hand and you never were the same
Since she is the goddess,
The fantasy you chase everywhere,
She is, an absolute beauty with a hint of madness

Ritvika

Young at heart as all should be. Poetic in life scenarios, replicating my natural talent and passion for writing and spilling down by thoughts on paper. A pen is your true friend as it never lies. In the final year of graduation from Hindu College, University Of Delhi. A girl next door, a sole lion standing in the jungle of wild masked humans and also a lover of meaningful social interaction. Hobbies include all the creative things one can experience while alive and breathing.

INSTA: @ritvikawrites and @ritvika_

Live For Yourself and See

Live for yourself and see,
Say, I will do this for me.
Neither selfish it is nor is it bad,
If others get upset let them be mad.

It's only you who is there for you all your life,
Put yourself first sometimes,
Doesn't matter if you are a sister, brother, mother, father or wife.

Live for yourself and see,
Say I will do this for me.

Standing there in the darkness searching for a shoulder,
No sign of any other, only your soul tells you to be bolder.

Live for yourself and see,
Say, I will do this for me.

Smarter These Toddlers Are

You say kids are like clay who need to be modelled by us adults,
You say they are naive and have to be guided by us adults,
I say they are more mature,
They know the real meaning of life.
They find happiness in little things,
No matter whatever for them you bring.
They don't discriminate on the basis of looks or race,
They smile and admire every face.
They don't over smart anyone for their own good,
Meanwhile we adults have our real face hidden behind a hood.
They express emotions of love or sadness,
Not like us saying "we are fine ", hiding all the madness.
The actual lessons should be learnt from them.
Stop your eyes from admiring the fake glitter,
Don't you see they are the real gem?

The Meaning of Life

I had everything but still felt incomplete.
Juggling between my busy life and my will to compete.
One day, I thought to take a break,
Leaving all the above at stake,
That day I laughed with my friends and family.
Bliss was a small picnic by the lake.

These little moments make you realise the meaning of life,
And how you are pointing a gun towards your head and
Stabbing your own self with a knife.
The more materialistic I became the more my life lacked meaning,
There was no one to love me and sip tea in the evening.

Now, I stop and slow down my pace.
Fearful I am, I don't lose the real experiences while running in the race.

Stop and stare at the nature.
The colourful life you long for is all present
Within this heavenly ecosystem.
Stare at flowers and feel the calmness within you,
Flowing in your veins.
It’s a miracle, we are a miracle, life is a miracle.
Grip each and every moment, don’t let it go.
Moments are like sand in your hands with your palms in a fist.

Trust Me, You Are Art

Not one work of an artist lacks grace,
Unique it is,
For every single one,
Beauty forms the base
Then why is the work of the almighty distinguished
Into what pleases the eye,
The next time you judge a person, darling,
Ask yourself why.
Breathtaking is everything the artist makes,
Who knew the canvas would be watched by venomous snakes.
The work of the almighty distinguished into what pleases the eye,
The next time you judge a person, darling,
Ask yourself why.

Harsh Dabarthala

Harsh Dabarthala is currently living in Australia and belongs to a small village Dabarthala (Karnal), Haryana. He passed B.A from Dyal Singh College Karnal. He is quite passionate about writing and most of his poetries are on love and life.
As a co-author, this is his second venture and much more will follow.

INSTA: @harsh_dabarthala

Chlo chalte h tarron k desh m...
Zor to bohot lgaya pr har gye hum zindgi ki race m.
Dushman toh bohot the pr apno ka tha Sahara.
Pta lga k vo sb to dushman hi the apno k bhesh mm.
Chlo chlte h tarron k desh m

Tu pyaar h mera, m diwana hun tera lakh diwano m..
Amir dil vale hmesha jopadi m hi milte..
Dil k gareeb hote h vo jo rhte h bde bde mkano m..
Agar ab bhu na smjhe to mit jaoge dunia se..
Tumhari dastan tk bhi na hogi, sbhi dastano m

Kabhi Dil Ke Paas Koi aane Na diya,
Par Tu karishma kar gai ajab sa
Tere Didar Mein Baithe Rahte Hain
Tu Jadu Kar Gai Gajab sa

Paida Hua to hath Jigar Mein Rakhe hue the
Na Jaane Ham kab se kisi par Mare hue the

Uska Pyar Uske vadon Ki Tarah Jhutha tha
vo majak Karke Chali Gai per Mera Dil Tuta tha

Vhh Bharose se Dekhe to Itna puchun Ki Main un pr Apni Jaan Nisaar Karun ya na karun..
Tu bhi mere Shauk ko Jarur Janti Hogi, tu ye Bata Meri Jaan agar tu mujhse Dil Mange to Inkar Karun Ya Na Karun.

Upar wale se Mang kar Laya tha Jindagi ke char din..
Do Aarzoo ke cut Gaye to Intezar Mein..

Jab Mulakat Hui Tujhse pata nahin plon ki vo kaun si ghadi thi
Ab To chamakna bhi band ho gai Ho Teri Yaadon Ki Ladai thi
Ham to Chahe Kitne Bhi Chhote Ho per Hamare liye tu Sabse Badi Thi Aur sabse Jyada yakin kiya tha Tujh pr
Lekin mujhe Marne walon ki line Mein Tu sabse aage Khadi Thi

Ke Tere Didar mein rahte hain Sari Raat
Khayal Tera Sone Nahin dete
Pata nahi Kiska Bura Kiya h Humne,
Jo Sapne Mere pure hone Nahin dete
Main Tera tha Tera hun Tera Hi rahunga
Tere Sath kiye the Vaade Aaj Bhi Kisi Ka Hone Nahin dete

Apne Halat ka khud Ehsas Nahin Hai Mujhko..
Maine Auron se suna hai ki Pareshan Hoon Main..
Gammo mein mohabbat k pd gaye Hain javani Mein..
Aur vo khte Hain Ki Nadan Hun Main..

Aisa Ittefaq Mere Sath hua
Unhi Se Mila hun unhi Ka Pata puchta hua

Unko Dekhe to a Jaati Hai Muh par Ronak
unhen lagta hai ki Harsh Ka Hal Acha h

Jab is fikar Mein Din Raat kt ti Hain Ki
Tumhen bhul jaye ya khud ko bhula De

Dhokha bhi usne Diya aur Hami pr Sara ilzaam Ho Gaya
Dil tutne Se thoda Dard to Jarur Hua lekin
Umar Bhar Ke Liye Aaram Ho Gaya

Mere Sanam ke Aate Aate Khat Ek Aur Likh Du
Main Jaanta hun vo kya Likhenge Mere khat ke Jawab Mein
sadiyan se Intezar Mein Hai Kalam is ummid par..
likhwaye Mujhse Khat Mere Khat ke Jawab Mein...

Ke Teri kamyabi Mein Hogi Tarif,
Par Teri koshish Pe tana Hoga
Tere Dukh Mein To bahut kam log Honge per
Sukh Mein Sara Jamana hoga

Teri Bhala Kaise Nibhegi Humse
Kyunki Hum to Dosti ko salam karte hain
Mein Unki Mehfil Mein baithana Pasand karta hun
Jo ghar ko fook kar,, Apne doston ke naam Karte Hain..

Koi mano ya na mano per ye zindagi to hone Barbad Thi
Aur kasmo Mein To usne Bhagwan ko bhi nahin chorda
fir Hamari kya aukat thi...

Hum unn par marte hain aur vo kabhi mere liye besbar Na Hui
usne Apni Nai Duniya bana li aur Hamen Abhi Tak khabar Na Hui

Mitne walon ko wafa Ka yeh sabak yaad Rahe
Bediyan Pairon Mein Ho Aur Dil Azad Rahe

Sangeeta Chauhan

This is Sangeeta Chauhan, hailing from Mumbai, Maharashtra, she is passionate about writing, she loves to write and ink her feelings, she has completed her graduation in Bcom, and currently she works as operation trainee for US tax documents verification process.

INSTA: @_.creative_quotes._

(1)

माँ...सीने से लागले मुझे
चलना नहीं आता
ऊँगली पकड़ कर चलना सिखा दे मुझे
माँ...सीने से लगा ले मुझे...
कही नज़र न लग जाए इसलिए
काजल की ढीठ लगा दे मुझे
माँ...सीने से लगा ले मुझे...
तेरी मुस्कान बड़ी प्यारी है माँ
तेरी हर मुस्कान की वजह बना ले मुझे
माँ...सीने से लगा ले मुझे...
अगर मैं गिर जाऊ कही
अपने प्यारे हाथों से उठा ले मुझे
माँ...सीने से लगा ले मुझे...
अगर में गलत राहू
तो डाट लगा दे मुझे
माँ...सीने से लगा ले मुझे...
सुना है जो प्यार करना माँ से सीखा है
वो कभी धोखा नहीं देता
तो माँ...प्यार करना सीखा दे मुझे
माँ...सीने से लगा ले मुझे..
सीने से लगा ले मुझे...

(2)

चुपके से मेरे सपने में आया करो
युही मुझे अपने सीने से लगाया करो
के भूल जाते है सारे गम कुछ पल के लिए
मनो मिल गए बिछड़े प्रेमी हरपल के लिए
चुपके से मेरे सपने में आया करो
युही मुझे अपने सीने से लगाया करो

करते रहेंगे बाते दिल की
न होना खामोश ज़रा भी
बस दिल की बाते मुझे युही सुनाया करो
चुपके से मेरे सपने में आया करो
युही मुझे अपने सीने से लगया करो

(3)

लम्हे लम्हे में तू
मेरे ख्वाबो के साथ मेरे सपने में तू
मेरे हर वो धड़कती धड़कन में तू
जैसे कोई अंधरे में भटके उजाले में तू
बस तू ही तू इश्क़ की आशिकी में तू
हर दफा हर जगह बस तुझको ही देखू
ये लफ्ज़ भी कम पड जाती
इसलिए मेरे डायरी के पन्ने पन्ने में तू
मेरे डायरी के पन्ने पन्ने में तू

(4)

मौत तू जवाब दे कुछ सवाल उठ रहे है
उन सवालों को संभाल ले मौत तू जवाब दे...
कुछ बात न कह सका इसका तुही हिसाब दे
मौत तू जवाब दे...
कितना सेह पता मैं इन दुनिया को तू ही बता दे
मौत तू जवाब दे...
घुट घुट कर जीना पसंद न आया
इसलिए मैंने मौत को गले लगाया
मौत तू जवाब दे...

(5)

कुछ पल ठहरे से ह

कुछ पल ठहरे से है मेरे ख्वाबो में जिसपे
न कोई सवाल,
न ही कोई जवाब है
है तो बस एक दुनिया,
जिसे हम ख्वाब-ए-ज़िन्दगी कहते है
जहा हर वक़्त, होती है मुलाकात उनसे
जिसने मेरे ख्वाबो की दुनिया सजाई है,
"के न कोई शिकवे न ही कोई शिकायत,
बस मिला है मुझे एक फरिश्ता ऐसा
मनो रब से मिली है हमे इनायत"

Manpreet Bhullar

Manpreet Bhullar belongs to a small village of Bathinda. He completed his secondary education from Bathinda and completed his graduation in Business from one of the colleges in Toronto. Currently he is doing a job as a truck driver and sometimes he expresses his thoughts through poetry. This is his first venture and he got the chance to present his thoughts to the readers and if he gets a positive response then it would give him dynamic energy to explore his thoughts widely.

INSTA: @manpreet3694

Asi Munde thode j sakhat hune a
Jiwe sanu chote hundya dsya janda,
J asi ronde dis jayiye ta fr sade te hssya janda,
Kyuki munde ro ta skde ni na ,
Ro pye ta fr kmjor mnne jawage,
Kmjor ta asi ho hi ni na skde,
Te hanju ta sadi akh cho cho ni na skde,
Sadi khasiyat hundi a k ,
Choti ji gal nu wdha chda k dher kr dine,
Pr jdo dil tutda na fr ajj kall prso keh k
Naldya nu v dassn ch der kar dine,
Jdo gussa aunda ta odo hi ose tym hi kadh dine a,
Par jdo pyar dikhauna hunda ta gal kal te chad dine a,
Asi ghrde halaat dekh k khaab laine a,
Mushkil aarthik, smajik ja kiho ji v howe
Asi sabh sambh laine a,
Asi padh likh k naukriya lagg k te fr viah kraune hunde a,
Kehn nu ta kuj mrzi kehlo par asi v smaaj de
bnaye riwaj nibhaune hunde a,

Asi barf de sakht tukde parwar nu garmi to bchaun lyi khurde hune a,
Asi oh hune a jo ghr da khyal dimag ch rkh k footpath te bahr ali side te turde hune a,
Sadiya v satkh shklla piche ik bcha dekhn di koshish kro,
Sab jhuthe bewafa ta asaani naal kh dinde,
Par koi wafa te pyar sche nu v dekhn di koshish kro,
Sanu v kllya nu dar lgda te band hnere kmre ch sau ni skde,
Te last te m khuga k juth bolde ne oh lok
Jo khnde ne k munde ta ro ni skde

Reeti- rewaz jo chalde c smaj ch,
Mai ohna nu mitauna chaunda c,
Tainu tere nalo wadh k mai tainu chauna chaunda c,
Tu muslim ghar jammi mai munda jatta'n da,
Par tainu viah ke ghare laiuna chaunda c,
Duniya'n dushman ashiq loka'n di jiwe kehnde hunde a,
Dila'n dula'n ch ta thik a,
Par hakikat ch thoda ashiq kathe rehnde hunde a,
Itefaq nal j kde kathe ho v jande,
Ik duje nu muhre vekh kina khush rehna c,
Viah ton baad Jo 2 chote chota niyane hone c,
Ik ne waheguru, ik ne allah kehna c
Ik ne waheguru, ik ne allah kehna c

Tu mushkila mushkila krda ae,
Apne asse passe vekh
Duniya dukhi to dukhi pyi
Awe kos na apne lekh,
Har kole dukhde snauna ne
Har ik nu ro vikhauna ae,
Muskurahat ohna di padh k vekh,
Jo dukh andar dabbi baithe ne,
Oh kde roya nhi krde,
Jina sachi dukhde dekhe ne,
Jinu v tu milda ae hass k mil
Ro k milega oh milno hat jange,
Jede sahare tu nitt ginda rehna,
Oh holi holi ghat jange
Chadhde nu hundiya ne slama,
Is gal nu dimag ch lai k chal,
Apna mada passa lako Te chnge nu
sahmne lai jiun da sikh lai wall,
Negativty to jiwe sare passa watde,
Bimar bnde to sare door ho khad de,
J tenu lagda tenu dukhi dekh koi tera dukh wanda reha,
Bholya panchiya chaj nal vekhega ohi tera mzak bna reha
yea,
Khud te ykeen rakh jina sikhla, jini cheti ho skda,
Nhi ta sahare takda takda tu siweya'n wall nu ja reha,
siweya'n wall nu jaa reha yea.

Edar odar diya galla’n wall dhyan jano hatt gya e,
Shayer likhda c Jo kaafi hun thoda ghatt gya e,
Asii tarafdaar rahe hamesha ohna de,
Par oh faisle kar nirpakh gya e,
Te mai sunya hassde rehnde ne oh bin sadde,
Piche j jo bulla aya c hawa da, eh gal das gya e,
Waise ta besharam hai ‘bhullar’ bada hi,
Par oh kar sharamshaar tanne kass gya e.
Sutt ditte ne tohfe mere ditte sare de sare,
Par ditta sheyad c Jo choo ke ohh hje v unglann nall chakh reha yea,
Ohh apne muho'n kehnde rehnde mai khush mijaj Han bda,
Je yea gall sach hai fer oh bol bol ke kyu dass reha yea.
Saah chadeya rehnda ohna de khyala nu hamesha,
Oh santushat oss jagha Te, fer ohh kyu nass reha yea,
Sau chon ek hille mai mud v jawa...
Je kise ek hille mai mud v jawa,
Par hun ho chuki tauba,
Dil mera kar bas gya yea,
Dil mera kar bass gya yea

Modern

Mera wakt abhi nhi aya hai
Musafir hu mai abhi
Manzil mil jayegi toh
Daur lekar ayunga

Modern is a software engineer working in a Canada based Company and has done graduation in Engineering in 2017 from Panjab University. He had started writing just one year ago just before the pandemic started and his love for playing with words has made him a songwriter and so far he has released one song, named Propose in Punjabi language which is available on all music platform sung by Renuka Dhiman As a co-author, this is his First venture and much more will follow.
INSTA: @modern_likhari

Kabr: A Tale of Separated Love

Maut se tu to mit gya
Teri yaado ko mitau kaise!

Kabr ke us par to awaaz bhi nhi jaati
Aapne dard mai tujhe sunuau kaise!

Tere jaane ke baad Kisi or se dil lgau kaise
Lag bhi jaye To usse wafa kamau kaise!

Kabr ke us par to awaaz bhi nhi jaati
Aapne dard mai tujhe sunau kaise!

Teri kabr ke sath ,
Apni kabr bnwau kaise!

Zinda dafan hokar hi
Apni maut ka jashan manau kaise!

Ek ek pal jo tere sath jia
Use fir se Dohrau kaise!

Tere sath dusri dunia me
Jakr Mil jau kaise!

Kabr ke us par to awaaz bhi nhi jaati
Aapne dard mai tujhe batau kaise!

Neend ko fir se
Aankho me laau kaise!

Aa bhi jaye to
Chain se so jau kaise!

Pal pal tere baare
Me soch na pau kaise!

Teri yaado ke samundar me
Na dub pau kaise!

Kabr ke us par to awaaz bhi nhi jaati
Aapne dard mai tujhe Sunau kaise!

Aukaat

तू औकात औकात करता है,
बता तेरी खुद की क्या औकात है?

जो पुरखों से मिला तुझे,
क्या वही तेरी औकात ?

जाति पूछे तू मेरी,
तेरी खुद्दकी क्या जात है?

क्या तूने सोचा कभी,
किसने बनाई ये जात है?
ईश्वर से पूछ जाकर,
क्या उसने बनाई जात है?

इंसानों को इंसानों से
लड़वाने को बनी ये जात है

फिर भी जो पूछे तू,
बता दू मेरी क्या जात है !

कर्म से पहचान मुझे!
बस यही मेरी जात है
यही मेरी औकात है।

Pehli Mulakat

Kaise kabhi bas ik mulakat hi kaafi hai insan ko pehchaan lene me,
Bas ankho me shiddat ho jinke fareb ho hi ni sakta unke dil me

Mai baitha tha unke samne,
Vo baithe thi mere samne,
Thode sehme thode dare dare
Hum dono lag rhe the

Unka swaal kya hoga
mai soch rha tha
mai soch rha tha
Kya unke mann me bhi
Yhi swaal hoga?

Aankho me dekhne ki
Kuch himmat jutai
Fir kuch himmat usne bhi dikhai!

Palko ko utha kr ik dum se jhuka lia
sharam ke parde se dil ko usne chura lia

Unke labo se do alfaazo ka intzaar tha
mera mann un se kuch sunne ko bekarar tha

umeed unko bhi thi kuch tareefo ki meri or se
mere alfaaz na koi nikla ishq ka chanta laga zor se

Mujhe ki hue
Unse pehli mulakat
Aaaj bhi yaad hai
aaj bhi yaad hai

Naari Mai Ajj Di [A Song]

Naari mai aaj di, Kise to na dardi
Rava mai bekhof ni, Khof khaande lok ni

Mada je koi bole, fatkaar denni aa
Salike naal bole, satkaar deni aa

Ched je koi mainu fer, khair nio usdi
Mange maafi vaar vaar, Chaped jdo vajjdi

Naari mai ajj di, kise to ni dardi
Rava mai bekhof ni, Khof khaande lok ni

Chopper udaundi kite, Bullet chlondi aa
Modern mai naari modern, life vi jeondi aa

Tu geeta vich khadku, Mai reality ch khdkoni aa
Border te aa ke dekh, Morche mai launi aa

Naari mai aaj di, Kise to na dardi
Rava mai bekhof ni, Khof khaande lok ni

Raaste Ki Dastaan

Roz naye musafir se
mulakaat mai krta hu
unke har kadmo ko
yaado me rakhta hu

Kuch yaade vo dete hai
kuch unko mai deta hu
manzil ko unki mai
asaan kar deta hu

Vo bhatke na manzil se
ye Dhyaan mai rakhta hu
har ikk musafir ko
bada pyaar mai karta hu

Tu shayar jo aaya hai
meri baat sunkar jana
meri zindagi ki dastaan
sabko jaakar sunana

Manzil ki chaahate me
Raaste jeena mat bhulna
Safar e zindagi ka jaam peena mat bhulna

Flairs and Glairs, a platform by a student for the students. We are esteemed youth struggling to carve out our path for our future and we follow a basic mindset Since everyone is not born with all-round skills. Joining hands with people who are born to execute it with perfection is the best way to evolve. Self-Evolution is the need of the hour but, evolving as a community is what we strive for. The initiative as kickstarted by, Founder- Mr. Shubham Shah with the motive to utilize the skillset and talent of writing has now a team of 10+ people who are actively participating into newer forms of learning and discovering talents among youngsters. We Provide platform and services like Publishing opportunities, Open mics, Workshops, Hands-on training. Operating with Brand Name of Flairs and Glairs (Publication House), we offer the chance of elevating a passionate writer to an esteemed author With Brand name Teekhe Zasbaaat. We bring to you an opportunity to get accustomed with the Public Speaking and Presenting of Thoughts along with regular challenges to brush up your inking spirit. The newest initiative to extend our services we introduced in a new writing Platform- The Glittering Fables and Ink Over Tears.

We Choose to Fly Like A Falcon than to be

a Leg Pulling Crab.

www.ingramcontent.com/pod-product-compliance
Ingram Content Group UK Ltd.
Pitfield, Milton Keynes, MK11 3LW, UK
UKHW022004190726
13853UKWH00004B/1728

9 789391 302627